ROBIN™

FACING THE ENEMY

WARNER BROS. PRESENTS

A JOEL SCHUMACHER FILM ARNOLD SCHWARZENEGGER GEORGE CLOONEY CHRIS O'DONNELL UMA THURMAN ALICIA SILVERSTONE "BATMAN & ROBIN" MICHAEL GOUGH PAT HINGLE ELLE MACPHERSON

MUSIC BY ELLIOT GOLDENTHAL EXECUTIVE PRODUCERS BENJAMIN MELNIKER AND MICHAEL E. USLAN BASED UPON BATMAN CHARACTERS CREATED BY BOB KANE AND PUBLISHED BY DC COMICS WRITTEN BY AKIVA GOLDSMAN PRODUCED BY PETER MACGREGOR-SCOTT

DIRECTED BY JOEL SCHUMACHER

WWW.BATMAN-ROBIN.COM

WARNER BROS.
A TIME WARNER ENTERTAINMENT COMPANY
©1997 Warner Bros. All Rights Reserved

ROBIN™

FACING THE ENEMY

by Alan Grant

Batman created by Bob Kane

Little, Brown and Company

Boston   New York   Toronto   London

To my wife, Sue, with love and affection

First Edition

Library of Congress Cataloging-in-Publication Data
Grant, Alan.
    Robin / by Alan Grant. — 1st ed.
        p.   cm.
    "Batman created by Bob Kane"
    Summary: Having abandoned his secret identity as the costumed hero
Robin, Dick Grayson continues to encounter crime in his civilian life and
wonders what his future will hold.
    ISBN 0-316-17693-1
    [1. Heroes — Fiction. 2. Adventure and adventurers — Fiction.]
    I. Title.
PZ7.G7666435Ro   1997
[Fic] — dc21   97-5047

10 9 8 7 6 5 4 3 2 1

COM-MO

Published simultaneously in Canada
by Little, Brown & Company (Canada) Limited

Printed in the United States of America

ROBIN™

FACING THE ENEMY

PROLOGUE

With a muffled roar, the sleek shape of the Batmobile sped into the Batcave, its headlights probing the cavernous darkness. It slowed, turned, and came to a halt in its custom-built parking bay, and as the engine died away two figures got out.

Batman seemed little more than a shadow, his long cape sweeping the stone floor as he used the remote control on his belt to activate the cave's muted lighting. Robin's red, green, and gold costume reflected the lights' soft glow, and the teenager grinned as he reached to take off his mask.

"Scratch two villains!" Robin said lightly. "Boss Magoo and 'Dozer won't be bothering decent Gotham folk for a long time."

Batman nodded, but his eyes were grim as he removed his own cowl and mask. "Tonight was not a success, Dick," he said, calling the teenager by his real name. "We captured two dangerous villains — yes. But you disregarded

my order not to fight 'Dozer alone. And your hotheaded-
ness could have placed us both in danger."

Dick Grayson bristled as they walked together across
the cave floor, past the trophies Batman kept of his more
bizarre cases — a giant copper penny, a playing card of the
Joker, and a life-size model dinosaur. "Hey, lighten up,"
the youth said testily. "We caught them, didn't we? That's
all that matters to a crimefighter."

Slowly, Batman shook his head. "Not so, Dick." He had
stopped by the desk where his butler, Alfred, had left
drinks and a snack, but he made no move to pick them
up. Instead, he looked directly into the teenager's eyes.
"You're not going to like what I have to say."

Dick glared back at him. "Try me!"

"You don't have what it takes to be a crimefighter — a
hero." Batman's words were carefully measured. He'd
known for almost a month — ever since they'd defeated
Two-Face and Riddler — that this moment would come,
and he had prepared himself. "Physically, you're superb,
one of the best natural athletes I've ever seen. You've
quickly mastered the basics of martial arts."

"Let's cut straight to the chase." Dick grated the words.
"What's the 'but'?"

"But you don't have the mental attitude," Batman went
on. "You're hotheaded, arrogant, and you disobey orders.

If we go on like this, it's only a matter of time before one of us is hurt — or even killed — because of you."

"I've already watched my family murdered," Dick said harshly. "Who cares if I die, too?" Even as he spoke, he knew he was being unfair. Bruce Wayne — the man behind the Batman mask — and Alfred had been there for him when he needed them most; they'd shown him nothing but kindness and friendship.

"Being a hero is not about recklessness," the older man said softly. "It's not about vengeance, or hatred."

"And I suppose you're going to tell me what it *is* about?" Dick snapped.

Batman shook his head. "You have to discover that for yourself." He paused for a second before going on, his words hanging heavily in the cave's cool air. "Until then, I consider this partnership dissolved. Batman and Robin are no more."

It took a moment for the words' meaning to sink in. When it did, Dick's reaction wasn't one of regret, or even understanding. Hot anger bubbled up inside him.

"You can stay on at the Manor, of course," Batman was saying. "Perhaps we can get you into college."

Dick was no longer listening. Angrily, he grasped the R-symbol on his costume's breastplate and ripped it off. "Save your breath!" he rasped, holding up the lightweight metal symbol in his fist. "I've got what I wanted: revenge for my family's deaths! Being a hero was just something to fill in the time!"

He turned on his heel. "I don't need to be Robin. I don't need heroes. And I don't need you!"

Dick stormed up the stone-cut steps that led to the house far above, brushing angrily past Alfred. Only the butler saw the deep regret that flashed through Batman's eyes as he watched the boy vanish into the darkness.

Less than ten minutes later, Dick Grayson gunned his motorcycle and drove out of Wayne Manor carrying little more than the same small suitcase he'd arrived with a month before.

Dawn was breaking, but the beauty of the scene was lost on him. His insides churned with emotion: shame at his ingratitude, anger at Bruce's criticisms, and grief at the loss of his family.

The fun-loving grin that had characterized him as a child had disappeared when his parents died. He'd felt it returning, sometimes, during his weeks with the Batman. But now it was gone again, and his heart felt like lead in his chest as he set out to find a new life.

CHAPTER

1

Midnight. A dull, sticky heat shimmered off the streets of Gotham City. The air was heavy and oppressive with the weight of a storm about to break.

High above the concrete canyons, the rooftops still glinted in the patchy moonlight. But dark, ominous clouds were already starting to pile up on each other, as if keen to see the tension in the air released.

A gargoyle jutted out from the fortieth floor of a sky-scraper. Its weather-beaten sandstone face turned toward the heavens, its mouth open in a silent shriek. On its back, worn smooth by years of rain and frost, a slender figure balanced gracefully.

Dick Grayson stood as still as the gargoyle, gazing out over the city spread below him. His sharp ears and un-blinking eyes drank in every sound and sight. Neon signs winked on and off in broken rhythm. Traffic noise was a dull, faraway roar, punctuated every few seconds by the shrill blare of a horn. In a darkened alleyway, a single orange street lamp sputtered and fizzled.

Lost in his thoughts, eighteen-year-old Dick could have been carved from rock himself. In his mind's eye he was dressed in the costume of Robin, the Boy Wonder, swooping and diving between the buildings, the ground a dizzyingly long way beneath him.

He sighed softly. Only a week earlier, he really *had* been swinging through these same rooftops, with the legendary Dark Knight of Gotham by his side. *But did it really happen?* he asked himself now. *Was it only a month since I stood shoulder to shoulder with Batman, trading punches with Two-Face and Riddler, two of the most evil villains Gotham City had ever spawned?*

Dick remembered the freedom the nighttime acrobatics had brought him, the respect he had for his grim-visaged partner — and the feeling of controlled hatred as he fought the evildoers.

The life of all Gotham City had been at risk from the villains' murderous plans, but they had been defeated. Justice had seen that they paid for their crimes.

Yet the weight in Dick's heart was as heavy and oppressive as the air itself. For justice could never reverse the evil they had committed. The past was dead, and all the justice in the world could never bring it to life again.

Lost in his memories, once more Dick was at the

Gotham City charity circus. The lights, the smell of the greasepaint and animals, the expectant roar of the crowd, surrounded him. He had been the youngest member of the Flying Graysons, the family trapeze act whose gravity-defying acrobatics had the audience on the edge of their seats night after night.

"Hey, does that grin ever quit?" Dick's brother smiled. Three years older than Dick, and an athlete all his life, even he marvelled at his younger brother's prowess on the high wire and the bubbling good nature that affected everyone he met.

But the gang boss Two-Face had changed all that. Even as Dick defused the bomb Two-Face had set to destroy the entire circus, the maniac's gun-wielding goons had killed Dick's family — the mother and father who'd raised him and taught him everything he knew, and the brother who'd first christened him "Robin."

Countless times since that terrible night under the big top, Dick felt pangs of regret. *Could I have done more?* he asked himself. *I saved the crowd. Could I have saved my family?*

He shook his head, as if to clear it of the cobwebs of doubt. Deep inside, he knew it wasn't his fault. There was nothing more he could have done. Batman had spent long hours convincing him of that. But no words softened the dull, empty ache in the pit of his stomach.

In the distance he heard a low rumble of thunder, but he didn't let it intrude on his thoughts. Batman . . . he wondered where the Dark Knight was this evening. What heinous crime was he investigating? What hideous villain was he exposing to the bright light of justice?

Dick hadn't seen Batman for a week now, since the morning he'd stormed out of the cave. He'd found his own apartment in the city, decided he would forge a new life and forget about the old one. But even so, the costumed crimefighter's presence dominated the city he protected. Dick knew he was out there, somewhere, fighting his never-ending battle for good, seeking justice for those who needed it most.

Dick breathed deeply. Batman's mission was clear, he reminded himself. It was his own that needed shaping. What was he going to do with what remained of his life, or what little of his life Two-Face had left him? Now that his quest for revenge was over, Dick felt hollow. Let down. Deflated. Like when he was a kid and the birthday cake never tasted as good as it looked.

He'd thought his partnership with Batman had been a good one, but he'd been wrong. Batman didn't want a partner, especially not a teenager like Dick. And anyway, there was truth in the angry words Dick had spoken in the cave — for him, crimefighting *had* just been a way to fill in the time.

But if Batman had taught him anything, it was that you could never go back. Whatever happens, whatever the pain, the survivors must go on.

"What should I do?" Dick asked the question aloud, the words hanging in the thick air. "Now that my old life is gone, what do I do?"

As if in reply, a massive streak of lightning suddenly split the night. It sizzled so close that Dick felt his cheeks and hair bristle at its passing. The mighty clap of thunder that followed in its wake filled the skies and left his ears ringing.

With the agility known only to a practiced acrobat, Dick leapt off the gargoyle and onto the building's flat roof. "Guess that answers my question," he said, and almost grinned to himself. "First thing I have to do is get out of here before I'm soaked!"

He disappeared into the building's maintenance exit as the first fat blobs of rain spattered like little bombs on the concrete. He felt better — as if some of the tension inside him had been released. Just like the storm. But he was acutely aware that he still had no answer to his dilemma: What should he do with his life?

A few minutes later, Dick let himself out of an emergency door onto the street. He stayed close to the side of the building, where it was drier, as he hurried along the deserted street. Head bowed against the rain, he hardly even noticed the figure that passed him on the other side of the road.

Seventeen-year-old Nate Toomey was on his way home from a movie, a horror show that he had yawned through. But he'd sneaked in without paying anyway, so he didn't feel as cheated as he might have.

Nate didn't like getting wet — it totally ruined the cool hairstyle he was unsuccessfully trying to encourage — but tonight he had no choice. He was flat broke, and the subway police were running a dragnet on fare-dodgers. So he had to walk the twenty blocks to the project where he lived. But he knew a shortcut through a maze of small alleys that would cut the distance in half.

The rain had eased some as Nate turned off the main street and into the narrow alley. It was like walking into some eerie alien world. Vandals had smashed all of the street lamps except one, which spasmodically gave off a garish orange light.

Suddenly, Nate stiffened. A noise, almost a yelp, came from around the corner ahead of him. Then a voice: "Help!"

Nate froze, his heart pounding. He was tall and well-built, and knew how to take care of himself in a fight. But this could be anything. He tightened his fists, eyes squinting to try to make something out through the thin curtain of rain.

"Who's there?" he called out warily, ready to run if he had to. "What's wrong?"

There was a moment's silence, then the sound of running footsteps as someone pounded up the alley away from him.

"H-help!" He heard the voice again, and now he could pick out a crumpled heap lying against the alley wall. It was a man. Blood dripped from his nose and lip, and he had a hand out against the wall for support as he rose unsteadily to his feet.

"Thank God you came," he gasped. Nate could see him clearly now, on his knees, panting to get his breath back. "Some-somebody mugged me. He t-took my wallet, I think."

Nate didn't reply. His gaze was riveted to the brown leather wallet that lay near the man's feet. It had fallen partly open, and several twenty-dollar bills had spilled out, soaking wet where they touched the ground. And the wallet was bulging; there was a lot more in there!

"Couldn't get a cab," the man was saying. He was leaning back against the wall, dabbing at his nose with a handkerchief he'd pulled from his pocket. "Should've known better than to walk through here. Do me a favor, friend — I think I might need a doctor. Please, call the police."

Nate's eyes hadn't shifted from the fallen wallet. Obviously the man hadn't seen it; he thought the mugger had taken off with it. But mention of the police seemed to galvanize Nate into action.

His heart pounding, he bent, snatched up the sodden wallet, and ran off up the alley in the same direction as the mugger.

"Hey! Hey!" Nate was dimly aware of the man's shouts behind him, but in a few seconds he'd turned another corner and the sound was lost.

Nate felt almost light-headed as he ran and ran. He'd sneaked into the movies, and he'd cheated on the subway, and he'd swiped a couple of bucks from his mother's purse from time to time. What he'd just done was different. And somehow, it was exhilarating.

His feet splashed down in puddles, soaking his jeans to the thigh, but it didn't matter. Nothing mattered, except that he get home safe with the wet prize he clutched in his sweating hand.

The seeds of a villain had been born.

CHAPTER

2

Soaked to the skin, Dick almost whooped when he saw the welcoming lights of a diner across the street. He was still some way from the small apartment he had rented with the little money his parents had left him. It was exciting and scary at the same time to be on his own in the big city, and he was looking forward to being home. But right now a cup of hot, black coffee was just the pick-me-up he needed.

JOE'S DINER, he read as he crossed toward it. OPEN 24 HOURS. The building itself was low, long, and narrow, like a railway car. Surrounded by several much larger and newer buildings, the diner looked as if it had always been there, as if developers had just built around and over it.

The smells of coffee and hot waffles greeted Dick as he pulled open the door. But behind their warmth was an atmosphere filled with tension and fear.

Dick took in the scene at a glance. A young couple sat at

a window booth, both obviously afraid and trying not to look at the counter area. A large fat man stood with his back to them. He was shaking a clenched fist at a gray-haired old man in a white apron who sat on a padded stool on the other side of the counter.

"Your coffee's lousy!" the fat man was saying, his words slightly slurred, as if he'd been drinking. "I'm not paying for it! And to teach you a lesson, I'm not paying you for the two rotten burgers I ate, either!"

The old man frowned. "I've never had a complaint about my food in forty years," he said. "If you're refusing to pay because you're drunk, okay — I'll call the cops. But don't insult my cooking!"

"Call the cops?" The big guy almost exploded. He lashed out with a backhanded swipe, but so clumsily that he missed the cook completely and knocked a pot of coffee off the burner instead. Its scalding contents spilled all over the counter.

"Now look what you made me do," the fat man raged, reaching out to grab the old man. "I'm gonna —"

He broke off abruptly as Dick spoke from behind him. "That's enough, friend," the teenager interceded. One hand grasped the bigger man's collar, the other held his arm in a viselike grip. In one swift motion, Dick turned him around to face the other way. Recoiling at the alcohol fumes on the fat man's breath, Dick propelled him toward the exit.

Wedging the door open with his foot, Dick shoved the man outside, into the rain. "When you sober up," Dick said in a voice that brooked no argument, "you might want to come back and apologize."

The man staggered a little, and Dick watched for a moment as he reeled away along the street, muttering curses under his breath. *Ironic,* Dick thought. *Even without a costume, I end up being a hero.*

As Dick turned to go back inside, the couple squeezed past him and hurried out, obviously glad to be saved from any further unpleasantness but determined not to stick around.

Dick walked back to the counter, where the old man was mopping up the coffee. "Are you all right, Mr. —?"

"Joe," he said. "Everybody calls me Joe. Always have, always will. Except skunks like that drunk. Insult my cooking? Hah!" Joe made a theatrical gesture, his indignation almost comical.

"He's gone now, and I don't think he'll be back," Dick assured him, but the old man just raised a disbelieving eyebrow.

"I'm forgetting my manners," he told Dick. He poured coffee from a second pot. "Thanks. Least I can do is give you a cup of coffee. Drunks, addicts, teenage thugs, gangsters — everybody thinks they can take advantage of an old man!"

Dick took a sip from his cup. "You should give up working nights," he suggested. "I bet your day manager doesn't get this trouble."

"No. And that's why he won't work nights. Nobody wants this trouble!"

The man paused, his head tilted a little to the side — almost like a bird, Dick thought. "Say," Joe went on, "you're not looking for a job, are you?"

"We-ell . . ." Dick's voice trailed away. The truth was, he *was* looking for a job. The expenses of the funeral had eaten up much of the cash his parents had left him, and the apartment took care of the rest. Dick knew that Bruce Wayne would lend — or even give — him any amount he needed. But what way was that to start an independent life?

"Yes, I am looking for a job." Dick had been brought up never to lie, not even to spare hurt feelings. "But I'm a trained . . . athlete. I wasn't thinking of working in a diner!"

"An athlete, huh? Well, everybody has to start someplace," Joe told him. "Albert Einstein — so I heard — got the idea for relativity when he was working in a fast-food diner!"

Dick laughed, and Joe pressed home his advantage: "What do you say? Money's not great, but the food is. Besides, you could leave whenever you felt like it." Joe hoisted himself back up on the high seat behind the cash register and played his trump card. "And you'd be doing an old man a big favor."

Dick shrugged. Okay, so this wasn't what he wanted out of life. But then again — he didn't know what he *did* want. Maybe Joe's offer was an omen. Joe might like to gripe, but Dick could tell from the outset that here was a man who enjoyed his life. And anyway, he didn't have any better offer.

"You've got yourself a new employee, sir," he told the delighted old man. "But I warn you — it's only temporary. The kind of mood I'm in, I could leave at any moment and just drift on."

"Spoken like a true bigshot wannabe," Joe said with a grin. "It's a deal. You work, scare off the bad guys, I cook and pay. No other commitments, right?"

They shook hands, and sealed the bargain with another cup of coffee.

Nate Toomey lived with his parents in a fourth-floor apartment in a small, compact project. Not a great place to live, but by Gotham standards it wasn't too bad at all. If Nate hadn't had to put up with his parents, he might not have minded so much.

The rain had stopped by the time Nate got home. He

went around to the small yard at the back of the block. Satisfied that no one was watching, he quickly climbed up the drainpipe that passed close to his fourth-floor bedroom. He'd sneaked out earlier, without his parents' permission, and he didn't want to face them now. They were always getting on his case these days, especially since Dad had lost his job. Now he was at home all day while Mom went out cleaning.

Nate had left school a year earlier, but he'd never worked in that time. To tell the truth, he'd never really looked for a job. Without qualifications, without any particular interests, the best he could get was fast-food or factory work, and Nate knew he could never do that. He harbored vague dreams of being a rock star one day, though the one time he'd borrowed a guitar he didn't have the patience to learn to play it.

Quietly he slipped in through the bedroom window. Surrounded by posters of rock and sports stars looking down from the walls, he took the stolen wallet from his pocket and spread its contents on his bed. His heart was racing, and he kept listening for the knock at the door that would show he'd been followed or the police had tracked him down.

There were seventeen twenty-dollar bills, and a five. Three hundred forty-five dollars! More than Nate had ever seen in his life. *The guy must have just been paid, or won at the casino, or something,* he thought gleefully.

It's not really yours, his conscience told him, like a small voice deep inside his mind. *You stole it!*

Nate pushed the nagging voice aside. It was true, he *had* stolen it — and from an injured man, at that. But, he reasoned, the man would have lost the wallet to the mugger anyway if Nate hadn't come along. That made him feel better. Yes, in fact, the man might have been even more badly hurt if Nate hadn't interrupted the assault. Why, the guy should be downright grateful to him. He should have *given* him the money as a reward!

Nate ran a hand through his wet black hair, for once not bothered by its spiky tufts. Three hundred forty-five dollars . . . man, he could buy a guitar and an amplifier . . . or a CD player . . . or maybe he could get some clothes, like those hot sneakers he'd seen in the Wayne Mall.

He started as he heard a noise in the hallway. Hurriedly stuffing the wallet and money under his mattress, he felt terror seize him. What if it was the police? What if the guy had identified him? It had been raining, but it was possible. He was a thief now. If they caught him, he'd be punished.

Then he recognized the shuffling footsteps of his father, up for a glass of water, regular as clockwork. Nate hardly breathed till his dad had gone back to bed.

I'll have to ditch the wallet tomorrow — away from the house, so there's no evidence to connect me with the crime, he mused.

He lay on top of the bed, fully clothed, senses alert for the slightest sound. *Being a crook can't always be like this,* he thought. *Worrying about everything, trying to get rid of the evidence, scared you'll get caught . . .*

Then he thought back to the thrill he'd felt when he'd first taken the wallet. Just remembering it made his adrenaline surge again.

It was almost three in the morning before he finally dozed off, with dreams in his head of money, flashy clothes, a big motorcycle, and an electric guitar.

In contrast, Dick Grayson enjoyed the soundest night's sleep he'd known since his family had been killed. He wakened only once, in the small hours. For an instant he wondered where he was. And then it all came flooding back — he was in his tiny brownstone apartment, the parents and brother he loved were dead, and there was an ache in his heart that felt as if a part of him had been lost forever.

Out of nowhere, a memory sprang into his mind. Blue skies looked down on a family picnic in a meadow. His parents and brother laughed as ten-year-old Dick showed off his acrobatic skills in the limbs of a tree by the waterside. And they laughed even louder when the branch broke and he tumbled into the stream.

Just before he drifted back to sleep, an image of Batman flashed through his head, replacing the happy memory with cold reality. "How can anybody believe there's justice in the world?" was the last thought he had before dozing off.

CHAPTER 3

"**O**kay, so I was stupid with the money," Nate Toomey admitted to himself. Two days had passed and he was looking in the window of a secondhand store. Inside was a guitar and mini-amp that not long ago had cost $500. Now, though, the sign read SPECIAL OFFER — $295. If only he'd come here first!

He cursed under his breath as he felt the few bills left in his pocket. He didn't need to count them. Less than ten dollars. He couldn't even use it as a down payment.

By this time the victim he'd stolen from was just a vague memory, a guy who "got what he deserved" because he should have paid Nate for saving him. First thing he'd done in the morning was ride the subway a dozen blocks away from his house. He got out, dumped the empty wallet in a trash can, and took the next train downtown. He bought sneakers, he bought jeans, he even bought a pair of shades. Nate didn't let himself think about it — he just pulled the money out and spent it.

He liked the look on the girls' faces when he'd breezed into the video arcade and bought sodas for everyone. Nate liked to be liked. It made him feel he was somebody, that he was worth something. So he bought everybody potato chips, too. And then somehow he was paying for ice creams and candy. With a start, he realized he had to leave while he still had some cash left. Without a word to anyone, he slipped out the door.

"No guts," that's what his dad used to tell him. "How do you expect to earn respect?"

Ha, Nate thought now, *what does he know? I spent three hundred fifty dollars in a couple of days! How's that for guts? Think those people in the arcade don't respect me?*

But how would he ever get that kind of money again? Things like that just didn't happen twice in anybody's lifetime. He needed a way to make money . . . lots of money. And he had to get it easily. Maybe his dad was right — maybe he did need guts.

So what if he became a thief? The idea scared him, but at the same time it attracted him.

Idly, his eyes drifted to the window display in the travel agency next door. Advertising their special "Africa Promotion," a huge color poster depicted a snarling lion crouched on a rock, about to pounce as a herd of frightened zebras raced by beneath him. The lion's fangs were bared, huge and drooling as it stalked its next meal.

Nate turned away, and watched a silver stretch limo with smoke-gray windows pull smoothly out into the traffic and accelerate effortlessly up the avenue. *Guys like that never have trouble,* Nate thought bitterly. *They get all the girls, all the cars, all the money they want.*

But how could he get that? How could plain old Nate Toomey ever connect with the serious money in this jungle of a world?

And suddenly it struck him, like a vision. The world *was* a jungle, and the people were animals. And most people were like the zebras in the poster — prey, to be stalked. Only a few ever became a lion, the stalker and hunter who gets the reward. The millionaires and the politicians and the gang bosses — that's what they do. Just like the lions, they find a segment of the population and prey on them.

That's what I'm going to do, Nate decided suddenly, as if the decision had been made for him by somebody else. *I'll find my target, and I'll jump on it. I will be the enemy of the people of Gotham.*

Inside the silver limo, billionaire industrialist Bruce Wayne settled back in the white leather seat and sighed.

He'd been working for ten hours straight, running his global business empire. He was tired. But he would enjoy no rest. The day's work was done; now he had to prepare for the long night as Batman.

"Did you make that call, Alfred?" he asked the stately chauffeur, who handled the large car with practiced ease.

Alfred Pennyworth didn't take his eyes off the road as he replied, "I did indeed, sir. Several times. But Master Richard is not answering his phone." A message had been left on Bruce's answering machine, giving Dick's address and number, but no other details. "Perhaps he's moved apartments, or even left town. You know he was in a highly emotional state when he left the Manor. He has no roots here, no real reason to stay in Gotham."

"That's why I'm worried about him," Bruce said softly. He put his hand to his forehead as he remembered his own parents, mercilessly gunned down by a mugger before his eyes when he was only five years old. He could never forget. It had been his frustrated desire for revenge that had led to his donning the mantle of the Batman, symbol of justice, destroyer of oppression.

He knew how Dick must be feeling. But he also knew only time can heal such wounds — and even then, never completely. Dick was an intelligent, personable, athletic young man. Bruce hated to think of him wasting his life when he had so much promise.

Bruce remembered standing on a rooftop with the boy after they had defeated Two-Face in their crimefighting aliases. Dick had been sad then, unable to comprehend that the tragedy that had befallen him would last forever.

"We can't bring back the past," Batman had said. "No matter the pain, the survivors must go on."

He hoped that the boy had taken that lesson to heart. In this world of temptation, it's all too easy for someone to fall off the straight and narrow track.

"Dick Grayson has a lot to offer the world," he told Alfred now. "If only he can find it in himself."

"Then let's hope he's out for a jog, sir," the butler replied in his rich English accent, "and not running away!"

"Keep trying, Alfred. I won't be happy until I know he's all right."

The limo surged toward the beltway, jostling for position with the expensive vehicles headed for their luxury homes in the wooded hills outside the city. Bruce Wayne put all thought of Dick from his mind. In less than an hour he'd be returning to Gotham . . . as Batman. He needed to focus all his energies on his mission: to clear the streets of crime, wherever it may occur. Nothing could be allowed to interfere with that, not even friendship.

Dick *had* been out jogging the first time Alfred called. He'd spent his whole life honing himself into a precision acrobat; to stay like that required training and self-discipline, or his skills would quickly deteriorate. So he set up a routine to give himself as broad an exercise base as he required. Who knew when his physical capabilities might be needed?

The second time Alfred called, Dick was shopping at the deli around the corner. And the third time, he was on his way to Joe's Diner and his first night's employment.

"Nate Toomey, what on earth are you doing in that bedroom? Come and watch TV with your dad and me!"

"Leave me alone, Mom," Nate snapped. "I'm . . . studying!"

His mother rattled the doorknob, but he'd been able to lock his door ever since he was sixteen, and it was locked now. *Good thing, too,* Nate thought, looking down at his handiwork. He'd removed the studs and labels from his black leather coat. His new sneakers were dyed with black polish. His black jeans were skintight. And he'd spent the last of his money on a thirty-foot lightweight rope with a metal grapple on the end.

He'd used a sheet of soft black leather to make a mask,

carefully cutting out twin eyeholes. Quickly, he dressed in his new outfit and pulled the mask over his head, securing it with the drawstring he'd inserted. He glanced in the mirror that stood on his dressing table, and started back, momentarily shocked by his own reflection. Then he laughed to himself. *If it scares me, how's it going to make my victims feel?* he thought with satisfaction.

Quietly, he slipped open the window. Below him, the backyard was overgrown with weeds and piled high with junk, including the remains of a car somebody once had left in the street.

He clambered down the drainpipe and dropped into the yard, skirting the trash as he headed for the lane behind the houses. He'd played in that car shell for weeks when he was a kid.

But he wasn't a kid anymore, Nate told himself impatiently. He was the Enemy. He was a predator. And he was going out into the night to hunt down his prey.

CHAPTER
4

The next week, Dick worked every night at Joe's Diner. Much to his surprise, he found that he enjoyed it. There was a hard core of regular customers: Bill the insomniac, who sometimes sat in the corner all night; the Agnew sisters, who sang a late gig at a bar and always came in for coffee afterward; Angela and Rodney and a half dozen other young actors and actresses from a nearby theater; and the cleaners and drivers and delivery people who kept the city running while its citizens were asleep.

Some of them were kind, some crabby; some polite, others as rude as any he'd ever met. But they were all people, and as Dick went about serving them, cleaning up after them, making sure they got what they ordered, he learned to look at them in a different light. Okay, so on the surface they were all different. Bill was moody and depressed, Dave the driver was always telling vulgar jokes, Sheila

Agnew had a high-pitched laugh that Dick often feared would shatter the cups. But under the skin they all had the same hopes and fears, the same ambitions and dreams. They wanted happiness, and love, the chance to enjoy themselves . . . the same as people everywhere.

Joe complained a lot, but in a humorous sort of way, and Dick knew he must love the life, really, or he wouldn't have been doing it for forty years. "Nah, it's a habit," Joe said gruffly. "I just can't get out of it. For a lot of my customers I'm like a doctor, or a social worker, or the family they don't have. Somebody to talk to, to confide in, to share the little highs and lows that make up life. What would they do if I quit?"

Dick's fourth night was a Saturday, the busiest of the week. Even after midnight, the diner always had a couple dozen customers. Dick had already proved to Joe he was a good worker, serving tables, washing up, lugging heavy crates of supplies as if they weighed nothing. But Saturday was when his other talents were called upon.

Dick noticed the guy as soon as he entered — cropped hair, a scar on one cheek, a thick silver ring on every finger. Dick wasn't one to judge by appearances, but there was a cold glint in the man's eyes that made him wary. Joe was holding court from his favorite chair, haranguing one of his regular customers about something. Dick delivered the stack of waffles with maple syrup and ice cream — amazing what folks want at one in the morning! — and turned back to the counter for the drinks.

Scarface was talking to Joe. "I got no money," the old man was protesting, but Scarface was insistent.

"Everybody knows about your secret stash!" He reached into his jacket and pulled something out. Dick stared in disbelief. Dangling by its tail from thc man's fingers was a dead rat!

"That's how you'll end up, if you don't *pay* up!" Scarface sneered, and threw the rat's body down on the counter.

The guy turned to leave. Dick stepped in front of him, intending to confront him about his action, but with no warning Scarface shoved him back hard and ran out the door. Dick stumbled over a diner's feet and went down in a heap on the floor, his metal tray clanging like a bell as it hit a tabletop.

"Sorry, sorry," Dick mumbled to the customer as he got up and hurried out the door.

He saw Scarface run across the street, and started to go after him. But just then the traffic light turned green, unleashing a flood of taxis and cars. Dick had already begun to run, and as the traffic bore down on him he had to make a split-second decision. Return to the pavement, and risk losing Scarface completely — or go for it. Dick went for it.

A car came straight at him, horn blaring as the impatient

driver thumped it with his fist. But Dick's long circus training had taught him to block out everything and concentrate on the task at hand. He leapt into the air, his left foot coming down on the car's hood. He saw the driver's surprised face, his mouth twisted in a curse as Dick sprang away again.

His leap took him onto the roof of a black sedan. Swaying, he extended his arms to steady himself as the car rounded a corner. He kicked off with both feet, and with outstretched arms just caught onto the stout metal casing of a hanging sign. Using the momentum he'd gained from his leap, the boy swung once, then back, then forward again, kicking hard for extra height. At the exact apex of his swing he let go, his body curving through the air gracefully to land on the curb a few yards in front of the fleeing Scarface.

"Going somewhere?" Dick asked. A look of surprise, then anger, crossed the other man's face. His hand shot into his pocket, and Dick's eyes narrowed as he saw the glint of steel. A switchblade!

Only a half dozen blocks away, the Enemy crouched on the roof of a low maintenance shed. His black costume blended into the shadows, making him invisible. He was taking long, slow breaths in an effort to calm himself, but his heart raced like a trip-hammer.

For three nights now he'd crouched here, watching the alley that ran along the back of a magazine and newspaper kiosk. Each night, the middle-aged woman who ran the booth bagged her money and took it to the bank's night safe. It was a five-minute walk — but she shaved it in half by cutting through the alley.

"You make a plan, you have to stick to it," Nate was repeating to himself. Because as the minutes dragged by, and the time drew nearer for the woman to close up, it almost seemed as if his legs were turning to lead weights. "You're the Enemy," he reminded himself. "People must fear you."

He thought of the money she'd be carrying, and that made him feel a bit better. Five hundred bucks or more, he figured. And she got that much every day; she wouldn't miss one day's takings. Besides, she was probably insured.

Nate stiffened as he heard her approaching footsteps.

Instinctively, Dick stepped back as Scarface swung the sharp blade in a wild arc. He remembered the rules of combat Batman had taught him — disarm your opponent at the earliest opportunity. Dick didn't give the man a chance to swing again. As he swayed nimbly back, the intended blow missing him by a full foot, he drove the flat edge of his hand into the man's arm.

Scarface snorted with pain and dropped the knife. Dick didn't wait to see if the man had any other weapon. His fist shot into Scarface's stomach, doubling him over. Before the villain could straighten up, Dick had the man's hands in a painful wristlock behind his back.

Ignoring Scarface's protests and the stares of passersby, Dick frog-marched him back to the diner and hustled him inside.

"What's this all about?" Dick demanded. Scarface was sullenly silent, and Joe looked uncomfortable.

"He was trying to extract protection money," the old man said. "But I told him I won't pay!"

"Have you called the police?" Dick asked.

Joe shrugged. "What's the point? It's my word against his."

Dick opened his mouth, ready to argue. But then he shrugged. This was Joe's diner. He was the boss. Curling his lip in contempt, Dick pushed Scarface toward the door. "Get out," he said coldly. "And if you ever come back, I'll make sure you choke on your rat!"

Tap tap tap. Every footstep seemed to take an eternity. Then Nate saw the woman's shadow on the wall . . . and suddenly, he became the Enemy. He felt calm, at ease, alert. Everything seemed to happen in slow motion.

He rose from his crouch, swinging the grapple around his head. He'd practiced countless times over the past few nights, and now it was almost second nature. There was a crash as it caught on the drainpipe opposite.

The woman from the kiosk hesitated at the noise, blinking into the shadows.

The Enemy swung down, breath hot and labored behind the leather mask, and landed directly in front of her. The woman opened her mouth to scream, but no sound came out. She stood frozen to the spot with terror. *Faced with this sinister masked figure, who could blame her?* Nate thought. He remembered how easily he'd spooked himself when he looked at his costume in the mirror for the first time.

The Enemy grabbed the handles of the bag she held, and pulled it from her unresisting fingers. He had grabbed the end of the rope again and was hauling himself up it before she even realized what was happening. After he scrambled the last few feet onto the roof, the Enemy unhooked the grapple and sprinted off along a narrow ledge.

He was already disappearing into the rooftops when she finally found her voice, and screamed.

"I hired the right guy, eh, Dick?" Joe's voice broke the silence of the diner. "That was some stunt you pulled."

"I told you — I'm a trained acrobat," Dick said non-committally. Thinking back, he could see he'd been showing off a little, fired up by the thrill of the situation. *Just like when I was Robin,* he thought.

"See, most folks are honest and decent," Joe went on. "But there's a criminal element seeks them out and preys on them — like a mosquito, or a vampire. Ordinary folks need hotshot stunt-guys like you to help them!"

"What about the police?" Dick asked.

Joe shook his head. "They got murders, and arson, and robberies, and a million other things to take care of. I can't bother them about a guy with a dead rat and a few threats. You fixed him. He won't be back."

"Was what the crook said true? *Do* you keep a lot of cash on the premises?"

Joe settled himself onto his chair and poured them both coffee. "My daughter lives in Australia. I have three grandkids and a son-in-law who I've only seen in photographs. I've been saving my tips to go out there sometime — so I have a little tucked away in case I need it fast. Hey!" He slapped the table. "Maybe I could even go this year, if you'd be willing to run the place for the autumn while I'm gone."

Dick was surprised. "You'd trust me to do that?"

For once, the old man was serious as he looked into

Dick's eyes. "Son, I don't know what it is about you. You're clever, friendly, quick to learn. I get the feeling you're special. But there's something you're holding back. You never talk about your past. Now that's okay," he added hurriedly. "That's your right. But if you ever feel like unloading it, Joe's your man."

It was on the tip of Dick's tongue to blurt it all out — to tell someone else about the pain of losing his family, about his days with Batman, his brief life as Robin, his capturing of the villains. But he couldn't. He'd promised Batman he'd never say a word of their involvement to anyone. He had to keep that promise, because if he broke it there was no telling in whose hands the information would end up. Criminal hands, most likely.

If Batman's secret identity became known, it would be the end of the Dark Knight's crimefighting career.

Instead, Dick said, "Thanks, Joe. And I'll be your man. Which means — sure, I'd be honored to mind the diner for you. We'll soon see who misses your cooking!"

Ten minutes later, the Enemy was plain Nate Toomey again, locked in his bedroom with $623 and some change spread out on the table. He felt exhilarated, all the earlier nervousness channeled into a special high. So *this* is what living is all about!

CHAPTER
5

Nate decided to play it smart. Hanging around the video arcade just cost him money. He figured he'd hang out someplace else for a while . . . which is how he came to be sitting in Joe's Diner, nursing a cola, when the protection gang came back.

It wasn't just one guy this time. There were three of them, and two looked like they could go ten rounds with a rhinoceros. The slim one wore a white suit and called himself Shiner; he couldn't hide the contempt in his glare as he looked around the diner.

"What an awful place," he sniffed, in a harsh East River accent. "Hardly worth Mr. Bentine's involvement. Still, we must be thorough. If one place didn't pay its insurance, why, others might also think they could step out of line."

"You'll get nothing from me, no matter how many of you there are," Joe blustered. "I got no extra cash!"

Shiner snorted with derision. "Everyone knows about your secret savings, Joe. Mr. Bentine doesn't want all of it — only his routine insurance premiums."

Dick was serving the actors' table and feeling good because Angela was flirting with him. Then he heard the raised voices as Joe started to argue, and excused himself.

"Leave this to me," Dick told Joe, stepping in front of the old man. Completely ignoring the two goons, Dick stared right into Shiner's eyes and held his gaze. "You claim you're selling insurance?"

"That's right. Pay up, and nothing bad will happen to these premises. Guaranteed."

"You have a copy of the policy?" Dick asked. Shiner's expression went blank. Dick turned to the dozen or so patrons in the diner. "Excuse me, folks. I wonder if you would witness this? Mr. Bentine's insurance company is selling us a policy, yet he has no copy."

People looked over, then looked away worriedly as the thugs glowered back at them. Shiner's lip curled in distaste. "I don't like people who make a fool of me. I presume you're the same one who bounced Ratman last night. Mr. Bentine would like a personal word with you!" He snapped his fingers imperiously. "Rake! Bandor! Bring him!"

Just then the phone rang.

Everybody froze. It rang again. Timidly, Joe picked it up

and listened for a moment. "Um, it's for you," he said, and handed it to Dick.

"Master Richard — at long last!" There was no mistaking Alfred's rich English accent. "I must have called your apartment a dozen times before I thought of speaking to your landlord. He told me you'd started work, and gave me your number."

"Alfred?" The teenager was surprised. "It's great to hear from you, but your timing is way off! I'll get back to you later."

Dick slammed the phone down just as one of the muscle men's hands closed over his biceps. The boy tensed, ready to fight back, but then he saw the fear on Joe's face. Dick wasn't afraid of these goons, no matter their size, but it wouldn't be right to fight them in here, where the diner might get wrecked and innocent folks hurt.

The goon called Rake pulled back his fist and launched a short, explosive punch to Dick's midriff. The boy saw it coming; he tensed his muscles and doubled up slightly as the shot rammed home. It would have winded Dick under normal circumstances, but he rode the blow. Still, he knew it was best to conceal his strength. He let out a long gasp, then slumped against the goon.

Bandor and Rake half carried him out of the diner. Joe and a small knot of people followed. Nate Toomey was among them, watching everything with keen interest.

At the curb sat a gleaming white Mercedes, looking like it had just been driven out of a showroom. The personalized number plate read BAD1, and it belonged to Rafael Bentine, a man with his fingers in a dozen shady pies. As the hoods hustled Dick over to the car, the rear window slid noiselessly open. A sibilant voice hissed from the shadows.

"So you're the troublemaker. I give you a choice — move on, or we'll break every bone in your body."

"Is that so?" Dick straightened unexpectedly, shoving Rake back from him. "Well, I'll give *you* a choice, Bentine — leave this diner alone, or I'll personally guarantee you end up in jail!"

"Fix him!" Bentine hissed.

Dick dodged the two goons and jumped up onto the car trunk, sliding over it to land on the other side. The driver's window was open, with the keys still in the ignition.

Shiner should have been more careful, Dick thought. He reached in and grabbed the keys.

"Drop 'em!" Bentine cried. Dick just laughed. He spun away on one foot, the other rising karate-style to slam into Rake's belly as the big thug lunged at him. Rake sprawled back into Bandor, and as they became entangled Dick moved again.

His foot lashed out, but this time it smashed the car's front headlamp. He ignored the screech of fury from inside, and moved coldly, deliberately to smash the other light. As the thugs charged around the car toward him, he ripped off the expensive electronic side mirror and threw it back at them.

"He's wrecking my car!" Bentine was almost beside himself with rage. "Kill him!"

Easily avoiding an outstretched hand, Dick vaulted up onto the car roof, stamping down hard several times with his heel. Someone in the crowd outside the diner laughed, then broke off abruptly. Shiner had pulled a gun and was taking aim.

Dick moved without even thinking. Leaping into the double somersault routine he used to do in the circus, he spun twice in the air as the bullet passed harmlessly under him. Then his feet lashed out, taking Shiner in the chest with a loud whack, sending him back against the wall. The gun flew from Shiner's hand and he sank to the ground, unconscious.

Dick loathed guns. A gun had killed his folks. Guns were deadly. Once fired, a shot could never be taken back. Dick kicked the weapon with the side of his foot and sent it sliding into the gutter.

The two goons came at him, one from each side. Dick ducked low, then sprang up again. The top of his head took Bandor solidly under the chin with a crack that could be heard a block away. As the man sank to his knees, clutching his numb jaw, Dick rubbed his head. That had hurt him, too — but there was no time to stop and think about it. Rake was charging him, a blackjack swinging wildly in his hand.

Dick fell on his back, feet up. He caught Rake in the chest and sent him sailing high overhead, slamming against a lamppost with bone-jarring impact.

As he leapt to his feet, ready for the next assault, Dick heard the squeal of tires. A police car pulled up, its siren belatedly whooping into life for a couple of seconds before shutting off again.

Shiner and the two thugs were dazed and bruised. Dick strolled up to the Mercedes with the two officers as Rafael Bentine got out. He was a small, neat man with an almost babyish face. But when he spoke, his voice revealed his true nature.

"I want him arrested," he rasped venomously, pointing at Dick. "He attacked my friends and me for no reason. He committed serious damage to my new car!"

"You have anything to say for yourself, kid?" one cop asked Dick, while the other scratched his head, inspecting the dents and broken lights and mirrors on the luxury auto.

Dick nodded toward Shiner and the two bruisers, by now recovering and looking slightly sheepish. "They wanted to take money that didn't belong to them. They threatened to break every bone in my body."

"You beat all three of them?" the policeman asked, incredulous.

Belatedly, Dick realized the risk he'd run in teaching Bentine and his goons a lesson. Ordinary people can't do the things crimefighters can. Now he understood why Bruce Wayne so often acted the wimp; he could never take the chance of someone making the connection to his secret identity.

"I . . . I guess I got lucky," Dick said lamely. He pointed at Shiner. "He had a gun. You'll find it in the gutter over there. And if you need any witnesses as to what happened, there are a dozen over by the diner."

"All right, gents," one of the cops said to the gang. The police knew full well who they were, but it wasn't often Bentine's mob did anything stupid enough to give themselves away. "Let's go down to the precinct and get statements from you, check your gun license, driving license, birth certificate . . ."

Dick suppressed an impish grin as the foursome were bundled into the police car. He whistled to catch Bentine's attention, then tossed the car keys in after him. "You'll be needing these," he said. "To drive to the repair shop. I just hope you're insured!"

Chattering excitedly, the other diners watched till the men were driven off, then went back inside. Lagging behind, Nate Toomey sauntered in and ordered another cola. Though he sat casually in a back booth, his eyes never left Joe.

Joe moved straight to shake Dick's hand. "I can't thank you enough, son. It warmed my heart to see those thugs get their just deserts!"

"That's only the start," Dick said. "They'll have to appear in court, too."

Joe shook his head. "I doubt it. You'd need to get these folks" — he indicated the other diners, back at their tables — "to agree to testify. And they won't. Because Bentine would send goons to torch their houses or kidnap their children!"

"If you all stood together," Dick began, but Joe broke in. "Bentine would knock us down together! Believe me, son, nobody can take the chance that they'll be the victim."

"So the perps get away to practice their 'business' another day?" Dick said disgustedly.

Joe nodded. "That's the way of the world, son."

"Why doesn't somebody do something?"

Joe shrugged. "Like who? We're all just ordinary guys. We can't stand up to organized crime. The cops try, but they have a zillion other problems. They do say there's a guy" — Joe's voice dropped dramatically, almost to a whisper — "They call him the Batman. He's supposed to help folks when they need it. But that's a full-time job for a *thousand* Batmen! No, sir, I sure don't expect to see him around Joe's Diner!"

Mention of Batman made Dick remember Alfred's call. Too late to call back now, he figured. Alfred often stayed up half the night doing computer work for Batman, but 3 A.M. just wasn't a sociable hour. Dick yawned and picked up a dishcloth. "Excitement's over," he said. "Who's for more coffee? On the house, given the circumstances."

"I'll take it out of your wages," Joe said with a laugh, but Dick knew he wouldn't.

Nate Toomey ran his fingers through his spiky black hair, got to his feet, and slouched out into the night.

CHAPTER 6

Nate bought the guitar and the mini-amp. His folks were convinced he'd stolen them, until he produced the receipt from the shop. Then they wanted to know where he'd got the money. He spun a tale about finding a winning lottery ticket. They still looked suspicious, but it was enough to satisfy them. They didn't believe him, but they never suspected for one moment that their son had deliberately robbed people.

He even bought a *Learn Guitar in 30 Days* tutorial book. But he never opened it. He couldn't concentrate on playing guitar, or anything else except his next nighttime adventure.

Nate had discovered that he *liked* frightening people. He liked taking their money. It made him feel powerful. And even better — he could make big money doing it! Despite his best intentions, he'd spent nearly all his newly acquired cash at the arcade; somehow, when there were girls around, he couldn't stop himself from showing off.

Maybe I should get a girlfriend, he thought. *But then again, she'd just get in the way of . . . my secret.*

Your secret . . . ! As always, Nate snuffed out the small voice of his conscience the moment it popped into his head. He didn't like to spend too much time thinking about what he had done. It was easier to justify it to himself, saying that people were soft and lazy; they *deserved* to be preyed on. It was the law of the jungle, wasn't it? The strong always eat the weak.

Across town, Dick and Joe's conversation had taken a similar turn. "I'm thinking of buying a gun," the old man announced. "That way, nobody will put the hammer on me again!"

Dick wasn't happy about the idea. "Most gun-related injuries are caused by people who don't know how to use them properly," he pointed out. "You have difficulty programming the coffeemaker, let alone dismantling, cleaning, oiling, and loading a gun!"

"There's truth in that," Joe agreed. "But I'd feel safer. It's a jungle out there, Dick. The strong prey on the weak!"

"But it doesn't *have* to be that way," Dick protested. "People aren't evil because they're born that way. They make decisions about it. I mean, nobody forced Bentine's protection gang to be crooks. They could be working on a construction site!"

Joe nodded. "You're right, of course. It's that decision, between good and evil, that makes us human," he said sagely. "But I'd still feel safer if I had a gun!"

"Take it from one who knows, Joe — guns aren't the solution. You don't get a second chance with a bullet. I know that from bitter experience."

The old man saw grief wash over the boy's face. "Want to talk about it?" he asked gently.

Instinctively, Dick knew that the old man would understand. But Dick didn't want to talk about it. Not yet. Not while that cruel ache still underlay his whole life. "I'm still trying to come to terms with it," was all he said. He paused as he thought of another old man. "Mind if I make a phone call?" he asked.

"Master Richard!" Alfred's delight was obvious. Dick and the butler had hit it off from the start; Dick liked Alfred's dry sense of humor and his ability to always be one jump ahead. When your boss was Batman, that was no mean feat. "I was beginning to think you'd never return my call."

"Sorry," Dick apologized. "Too busy putting together

my new life, I guess." But he knew that was only part of the reason for the delay. His hotheaded anger with Batman had long since faded. Now, he felt kind of stupid that they'd ever argued at all.

"Master Bruce wouldn't thank me for saying this," Alfred told him, "but he was quite worried about you."

"Hey, nobody needs to worry about me! I can take care of myself!" Despite his friendliness toward the old retainer, Dick's guard came up automatically.

"Of that I have no doubt, sir," said Alfred tactfully. "But that doesn't stop your friends from wondering if you are all right."

Instantly, Dick felt ashamed. He owed a lot to Bruce and Alfred. When he was at his lowest ebb, they had given him hope. They made him feel that maybe, just maybe, one day life would be worth living again.

The conversation took a lighter turn for several minutes as Dick described his job and the fact that, strangely, he was enjoying it. "Must be because Joe reminds me a little of you, Alfred!"

Alfred coughed. "Hmph. I dare say running a diner is easier than running a billionaire industrialist who's also a super hero! Now — when can we expect a visit?"

Dick hesitated. He'd spent several weeks living at Wayne Manor. He loved it. And he *would* like to see Alfred and Bruce again. But . . .

"Angela, one of the girls who comes to the diner, asked me for a date tomorrow. We're going to the Gotham Island Funfair. It's the only time I have off. How about next week?"

"I'll look forward to it, sir." Alfred's voice became more serious as he continued. "This is a large house. Even billionaires and faithful butlers get a little lonely sometimes. Don't let me down."

"I won't," Dick promised. He would go. Next week.

That night, Dick had a nightmare. It was strange — he knew he was dreaming, but he couldn't change it. Almost as if he were a ghost in his own dream.

He was back in the circus, the smell of sawdust strong in his nostrils. The lights were bright, the crowd was laughing at the clowns, and his father was giving his family their last briefing before they performed their high-wire act. "Remember — leave your emotions on the ground," he told them. They knew the speech by heart; he said the same thing every night, like a ritual. But they all understood the sense that lay behind the words. Up there, where you depended on each other's skill for your very life, was no place for arguments, or jealousies, or feuds. Up there, only your expertise and timing were important.

Then Dick was swinging on the trapeze, higher and

higher, ready for the supreme triple jump. Far below, the crowd was deathly silent as his brother, dangling head down, legs hooked into the other trapeze, readied to catch him.

Higher still, until he thought he was going to take off for space. It was a sensation he loved and never tired of. But when he looked down from the top of his swing, the peak of the big top tent itself, he saw Two-Face and his thugs rush into the circus ring.

They fired indiscriminately as the madman gave his orders. One or two people fell, and the others panicked. The whole crowd rushed around, screaming, trying to get to the exit. Two-Face stood in the middle of the ring, laughing maniacally. Dick knew what was coming next. With a sick feeling in his heart he let go of the trapeze and spun crazily toward the sawdust-strewn ring far below.

He knew he was only dreaming, that it hadn't really happened this way, but he was powerless to stop it.

He landed lithely, directly in front of Two-Face. "Don't kill them," he pleaded. "They're my family — they're all I've got! Take me, but leave the others! Please!"

The insane villain paid him no heed, as if Dick were a phantom, of no substance at all. Two-Face pointed upward, then his goons were shooting. High above, a rope snapped and the Flying Graysons began their final, fatal plunge.

Dick watched, helpless to intervene. His mother

screamed, twisting in the air, making a desperate grab for his father's hand. They clasped — but there was nothing for them to cling to. Behind them, Dick's brother pin-wheeled his arms and legs as he plummeted. Tears stung Dick's eyes as his loved ones crashed to the ring and lay, silent and broken, as if they were dolls.

Dick woke in a cold sweat. It was only a dream! Then he remembered where he was. It was real. Just like in the dream, he felt tears fill his eyes. Two-Face and his thugs were parasites, like old Joe explained. They prey on decent folks, not caring what damage or injury they leave in their wake, not caring about shattered families and broken dreams.

He clenched a fist and would have punched the wall in sheer frustration if he hadn't remembered Batman's words. "We can't change the past. The survivors must always go on." Strange, how he was always thinking of things that Batman said. His words were like nuggets of wisdom that grew brighter with time.

Dick felt a tinge of regret. Despite their differences, he and Batman *had* defeated the villains by working together. Things hadn't been perfect, but who was to say they couldn't have improved, given time?

The teenager slid out of bed and pulled back a rug to reveal a loose floorboard he'd found. Levering it up, he reached underneath to retrieve something wrapped in heavy layers of polyethylene. He peeled the covering away, and for the first time since he stormed out of Wayne Manor, Dick gazed upon his Robin costume.

He'd taken it with him, unable to leave it behind even in his anger. Memories washed over him, and he sat there for a long time without moving.

Nate was picked up by the police at noon that day, on his way to the arcade. They put him in the car but made no effort to drive off, just sat there, both policemen turned around in the front seat to question him.

The hard-faced cop, Guinness, spoke first. "Somebody's been robbing folks around here. Dressing up in a fright mask and robbing 'em!"

"What else is new?" Nate said fliply.

"Whoever's been taking other folks' money," Guinness continued doggedly, "we thought — maybe he's been spending it. So we asked around the coffee shops, the bars, the arcades, and the pool halls. And what do you know, somebody said that kid with the spiky hair, Nate Toomey, sure has been throwing money around like water lately."

Nate's blood turned to ice, but he forced himself to stay nonchalant. Of course — he should have thought of that. Spending the cash in the neighborhood made him a suspect. If they had a warrant, they could search the house and they'd find his costume and what little remained of the money. He hardly heard the other cop say, "Make it easy on all of us, son. Just tell us — did you do it?"

"Excuse me?" Nate's voice was hoarse. "I don't know what you're talking about. I never robbed anybody in my life." As he went on, he started to feel more confident. "Sure I had some money to spend. But that's not a crime, is it?" He was starting to feel genuinely indignant, as if he really were innocent. "If that don't beat all — suspecting somebody of being a robber because he spent some of his own hard-earned cash!"

"So we're just wasting our time?" Guinness stared at Nate, but Nate didn't flinch. With a sigh, the policeman climbed out and opened the door. "Go on, then, son. Get out of here."

"But don't go too far," Guinness's partner warned Nate. "We might want to question you again!"

Nate felt triumph swell inside him. They didn't know anything. They were just bluffing. They had no evidence. But he was careful not to let them see how good he felt. He'd lied to the police and got away with it. The cops were just the same as anybody else — stupid, trusting, almost begging to be taken advantage of. But he was invincible, like a super hero!

"Glad to be of assistance, officers," Nate said graciously, smothering his smug grin as he got out of the car and sauntered off down the road.

The encounter had taught him something important, he realized. What if they'd called at his house! He made up his mind. He needed someplace else to hide the costume and his loot. And another thing — no more of these small-time stickups. He could spend five hundred dollars in only a few days. He needed something bigger, a score that would keep him living the high life for weeks. Months, even.

And Nate Toomey thought he knew exactly what that score was!

CHAPTER 7

The abandoned apartment block was set well back from Delaney Street. Most of the doors and windows were covered with rusting corrugated iron or plywood. Nobody had lived there for a decade; it was just another festering ruin, in a city that paradoxically was full of both empty buildings and homeless people.

This building provided a shelter for only one person now — Nate Toomey. He'd brought his money, his costume, and plenty of food and drink. He'd told his parents he'd be staying with a friend for a few days. He settled into a room on the tenth floor, just one story below the roof. He chose it for a very special reason. From its south-facing window, he could see down onto the street and into the facade of Joe's Diner.

If gangsters like Raf Bentine were interested in Joe's secret stash, you could bet it was a jackpot. And who better to win that jackpot than the Enemy? He'd seen what the old man's helper had done to the gang, but it just made him think Joe's stash must be even larger, if he'd hired a martial arts expert to protect it!

The Enemy was in no hurry to tangle with Joe's bouncer, however. But even bouncers need a night off, he figured. So he'd watched, unmoving, for several nights now, recording Dick's schedule. He arrived at 8 P.M. sharp and didn't leave till twelve hours later. *What a chump,* Nate thought, *working in a dive like that for a half day at a stretch!*

Chump yourself! his inner voice mocked him. *You're waiting here all night.*

"Yeah, but I'm doing my homework. And I'll be getting paid for it soon, in spades!"

The sixth night Dick didn't show. The Enemy crouched by his window, watching, chewing snacks, occasionally sipping from a soda can. An hour passed. As he became convinced that tonight was the night, he began to feel the way he always felt before he committed a crime — that weird mixture of anticipatory excitement and terror of being caught.

Another hour passed. The regulars came and went. No sign of Dick. It *had* to be his night off!

Just after eleven o'clock, the diner went through one of its periodic slack patches. There were no customers at all. It was now or never. The Enemy had become more bold with each crime he'd committed, but this would be his biggest yet.

He eased out of the window and slid down the rope he'd left hanging there.

Once on the ground he kept in the shadows, skirting pools of light from street lamps, as he raced toward the diner. The effort had him breathing hard. That was the only problem with the outfit — the mask got hot and airless. But it was worth its weight in gold for frightening — and that's what Nate intended to do now.

At the city fairground, the Big Wheel rolled, its lights flashing hypnotically as it carried laughing, screaming boys and girls in the air. In one of the baskets Angela, Dick Grayson's date, looked out into the distance at the city. "Look at all those lights," she gasped. "The city sure is pretty from up here."

Beside her, Dick nodded. "It's great, isn't it?" He didn't tell her he'd seen this view dozens of times, swinging through the nighttime rooftops with Batman.

Angela smiled. She liked Dick — he was kind and thoughtful, and he showed flashes of a really keen sense of humor. Good-looking, too, as her friends had pointed out when they'd dared her to ask him out. She was glad she'd taken the dare.

Invisible in the shadows, the Enemy peered in through the diner window. Just Joe, seated on his old chair, reading a magazine, drinking coffee. As swiftly and silently as he could, the Enemy slipped inside the door, flipped the OPEN 24 HOURS sign to read CLOSED, then hit the main light switch. The diner plunged into darkness except for the glow of the controls on the coffeemaker.

"Yes!" Angela squealed delightedly as the hoop she'd thrown fell down over a fluffy yellow duck.

She grinned at Dick as the stall owner handed her the prize, the fluffy yellow toy, which on closer inspection looked more like a dolphin from some alien dimension. "Think you can do better?" she teased.

But Dick didn't rise to the bait. The crowds of laughing, happy people had had a strange effect on him. He felt suddenly depressed, reminded even more acutely by the families all around him that he no longer had any family at all.

"Sourpuss!" Angela flounced away, cuddling the yellow thing against her. Trying to shrug the feeling off, Dick followed her.

A beam of light stabbed the darkness inside the diner. Joe had taken his flashlight from beneath the counter, and now he swung it to face the aisle. He gasped and almost dropped the light as it illuminated the figure before him in all its terror.

"Sweet mercy, what are you — ?" the old man cried.

"I am the Enemy. Your enemy — the enemy of all Gotham! Where's the money hidden?" Nate kept his voice low and, he hoped, unrecognizable. The cops had hassled him once; he didn't want them coming back.

"I — I don't have any money," Joe stuttered, "just what's in the register." The Enemy cut him short with an impatient curse and stepped closer to the counter.

"Liar! I know about your secret stash. Where is it? Show me, or else!"

"You'll never get it!" Suddenly Joe swung the flashlight back and brought it crashing down like a baton on the Enemy's head. Nate managed to raise an arm and ward off the blow, though it sent shock waves all the way down to his fingers. Joe raised the flashlight to bring it down again, but this time he was too slow. The Enemy lashed out with a gloved fist.

Even the Tunnel of Love couldn't snap Dick out of his depression. True, he did put his arm around Angela's shoulder in a halfhearted sort of way, but any fool could tell that his thoughts were a zillion miles away.

By the time their carriage emerged at the other end, Angela had firmly decided that handsome guys didn't necessarily make the best dates.

The Enemy's blow caught Joe on the side of the head. He staggered against the counter, and a stack of plates went crashing to the floor. He fell against his chair and grabbed at it, trying to steady himself, but it fell over with him. As the chair struck the tiles, its seat was knocked off by the impact . . . and a shower of cash came bursting out.

"Help! Help!" Joe called out as he struggled to get to his feet.

The Enemy panicked. "Shut up!" he rasped. His hand fell on a heavy glass ashtray. He swung it savagely. There was an awful crunching sound as the glass hit Joe's skull. Blood flowed from the wound. Joe gasped and slid backward. He tried to speak but the words wouldn't come, and he fell back in pain.

"I'm sorry. I'm not much fun, am I, Angela?" Dick said.

"I get the impression you're not really trying, Dick. What say we call it a night and go home?"

"You're sure you don't mind? I feel like I've let you down."

"Tell you what," Angela said with a smile. "I know a place where you can take me for coffee first."

"I warned you!" the Enemy hissed. "This is your own fault! You should have told me!"

He was down on his knees, scooping up as many of the bills as he could. Everything had gone wrong. This wasn't supposed to happen. He'd never meant to hurt the old man!

He ran from the diner, bills stuffed in all his pockets. Across the street he grabbed the end of his rope and hauled himself up it. He cursed as the grapple dislodged some debris from the rotting wall. But it held, and seconds later he was up on the roof. He lay for a moment, staring up at the sky, panting with effort. Then he yanked up the rope and headed for his secret hideout.

Dick and Angela's cab pulled up to the diner. They paid the driver hurriedly, both knowing immediately that something wasn't right because the diner lights were out. And Joe's was always open.

Dick held Angela back while he went in first. He groped

behind the door for the light switch, snapped the lights on, and stared, stunned. There had been a fight. The chair was knocked over. Broken dishes. Money scattered here and there.

Dick rushed behind the counter, then froze in horror. The old man was lying on the floor, his leg twisted under him. Blood stained the tiles around his head. An icy blast shot up Dick's spine.

"Joe?" His voice was barely audible. "Joe — are you . . . ?"

He turned to Angela. "Call an ambulance! And the police!"

He knelt by Joe's side, fingers gingerly feeling for a pulse in the old man's wrist. There was none. Heart sinking, Dick leaned over him, close to his face. There was no breath he could detect.

"Cancel the ambulance," Dick said quietly. Angela frowned, her hand on the receiver.

"He's dead," Dick whispered, and raised a knuckle to brush away the tear that threatened to cloud his eye.

Nate Toomey arrived home at 1 A.M., just as his father got up for his glass of water. "Boy, where have you been all this time?"

Nate mumbled some excuse and hurried to his room.

His emotions were in turmoil — terrified he'd be caught, but exultant that he'd escaped. He'd counted the money. More than three thousand dollars. He was rich!

But what would happen if the old man died? There'd be a murder hunt. Stealing was one thing, but murder —

I warned the old guy! He shouldn't have tried to stop me. It was his own stupid fault. But the old man's face, lit for an instant by the flashlight, came to haunt him each time he closed his eyes.

He'd been in fights before — fistfights at school, a couple of brawls at the arcade. Nate knew how to handle himself. But the old man hadn't fought back. He'd just crumpled, like a sack of bones.

Nate Toomey did not sleep at all that night.

CHAPTER 8

The police had taken statements from Dick and Angela, then taken Angela home. Dick stayed to lock up after the forensic team had finished dusting for fingerprints and looking for clues.

"I'm not hopeful," Lieutenant Kitch, the officer in charge, told him. "No prints, probably means the culprit was wearing gloves. Seems he did it for the old man's money, panicked and grabbed what he could." His eyes narrowed. "Who else knew about the money?"

"The whole neighborhood, it seems," Dick said wearily. "He was going to use the money to visit his family in Australia. He'd never seen them." A lump rose in the teenager's throat. "And now he never will."

He turned to the detective. "How could anybody *do* that? How could they kill a harmless old man?"

"When you've been around as long as I have," Kitch told

him, "you're never surprised by what people will do. It's usually for love, or hate, or money. Or a combination of all three."

Kitch offered Dick a ride home, but the teenager declined. He wanted to be alone with his memories of Joe, and his troubled thoughts. He walked, his footsteps echoing down the empty streets. He didn't know where he was going, and he didn't care. His mind was racing.

It seemed unreal that in this day and age, an old man could be bludgeoned to death for a few scraps of paper. And then Dick remembered all the other things — the muggings and thefts, the drunks, the gangs, the random violence. The victims were people like Joe — poor, honest, decent folks. What was it Joe had said? *Ordinary folks are like a host body, and all the parasites, the fleas and vampires and mosquitoes, they feed on us.*

Vaguely, Dick realized he was walking alongside a metal railing with an elaborate spiked top. He glanced up and saw with surprise that he was at the gates of Gotham Cemetery. It was a massive place that had been used for centuries to bury the city's dead. The street lamps were shaded by trees here, and in the moonlight the graveyard looked spooky and unwelcoming. Statues and carvings broke the skyline like a forest, alongside vases and urns and tombstones.

Dick started to turn away, but paused. He turned back. The gate was closed, locked for the night when darkness fell. But to Dick, climbing it was an easy matter. Seconds later he stood inside, and seconds after that he was picking his way among the rows of marble memorials.

He seemed to have walked a mile, and was beginning to think he'd become lost in the cemetery's winding pathways, when he saw it. A plain white marker, illuminated in moonlight, the flowers he'd left on his last visit starting to wither and die. On the stone were carved simple words: "For my mother, father, and brother. The Graysons fly no more. In loving memory, Dick."

They too had been victims of the parasites. Just like Joe. Like every other crime victim. Sure, Batman had tried to help. But Gotham was a city of eight million people. Even Batman couldn't be everywhere, couldn't help everyone.

Then why does he do it? Dick wondered. *It's a war he can never win. For every innocent person he helps, a dozen more will end up hurt. Why doesn't he just give in?*

And in a flash of sudden understanding, he knew. It was as if the words spoke themselves inside his head: Batman does it because he chooses to do it. Because the people need him. Because the world needs heroes. And if Batman *didn't* do it . . . then there would be even more pain, and misery, and hurt in the world.

Dick thought long and hard, and the longer he stood there, the more determined he became. He had reached a decision. He had made a choice.

And in that moment, a hero was reborn.

CHAPTER 9

Dick could have asked Bruce Wayne for help. In other words, he could have called in Batman. But Joe had been *Dick's* friend. That made it personal, something he had to sort out himself.

He'd only been Batman's partner for a short time, but it was enough for him to have learned that the foundation that underlies all good crimefighting is basic detective work. There's no point rushing into action unless you have a plan. And to have a plan, you need data.

The police were working on the case, of course, but Dick had no way of accessing any information they might have. If they'd come up with any clues, they were playing it close to their vests, because there was no mention of any leads on the TV news or in the papers, where Dick scanned every word written about the tragedy.

He thought of Joe's daughter, and the grandsons in Australia who would now never meet their granddad. He wouldn't let the old man's death go unavenged! There must be some way of tracking down his killer.

And then it struck him — Rafael Bentine. The man had threatened Joe. Dick had publicly humiliated him, cost him a lot of money on the auto repair, and messed up his strong-arm boys. It had to be Bentine!

A sickening realization struck him. If it was Bentine, Joe's death would have been Dick's fault. Perhaps if Dick hadn't acted rashly, hadn't shown off, Joe might still be alive today. Dick clenched his fist so hard it hurt.

Bentine wouldn't have done it himself, of course. That's why he hired goons. No doubt the cops would figure it out sooner or later, too. Dick knew he had to get there first.

He could hardly wait for night to fall.

"Your so-called friends have enough of you?" Mrs. Toomey asked, scowling at her son. "You haven't left the house all day."

Nate didn't look up from where he was slouched in front of the TV. "Just leave me alone!" he snapped. Wasn't that just like his parents? First they moan at you because you're out, then they complain when you stay in.

But Nate couldn't even be bothered arguing with them.

He'd heard on the news that the old man was dead. He kept seeing his face, and the little voice inside him said over and over: *You killed him! You killed him!*

Unable to shut the memories of last night from his mind, Nate got suddenly to his feet. "I'm going out," he announced.

"To look for a job?" his father asked dubiously.

"Yeah. Right," his mother said with dripping sarcasm.

Nate stormed out of the house, slamming the door behind him. He had enough whirling around his brain without his parents adding to it.

Unconsciously, he turned and walked in the direction of the diner. He stopped short on the sidewalk. They say a murderer always returns to the scene of the crime; he'd heard it on a dozen TV crime shows. That's how they always got caught.

Well, Nate Toomey was nobody's fool. He switched direction and wandered aimlessly for a while. He was sorry the old man was dead. Of course he was. But it was the old coot's own fault for fighting back. He shouldn't have. If he'd just given in, he'd be alive now.

Nate bit his lip anxiously. If the police pulled him in again, the questions would be harder to answer. They'd tear the neighborhood apart to get their killer. They'd grill his parents, search the apartment . . .

Better if I leave town for a while, Nate thought. *I can*

head out west, somewhere I'm not known — where nobody would care about a dead old man in Gotham City. Yes, his mind was made up. He was leaving. He'd stop by his hideout and collect his things. But it was far too dangerous to enter in daylight.

He could hardly wait for night to fall.

The last rays of the sun had barely set when a figure swung through the rooftops of the city.

High above the traffic, Robin soared like the bird for which he was named. His grapple snaked out, held; then he was swinging, landing on some ledge or parapet, his weighted line once more arcing into the night. It was like being back at the circus: with everything else blotted out, his entire attention was focused on the task at hand, knowing that only the smallest of slips stood between life and a plunge to the pavement hundreds of feet below.

Ahead was what he was looking for — the luxurious River Heights condo, where Rafael Bentine owned the entire penthouse floor.

It was a clear evening, and from here the Milky Way was just visible in the night sky. Bentine and his men were sitting in the glass-walled living room of his fabulous home, playing poker. They'd been charged with various violations of the law after the diner brawl, but Bentine didn't pay a sharp lawyer for nothing, and they were all free on a few thousand dollars' bail. The lawyer would appeal against any hearing, and generally delay things until the authorities gave up out of frustration.

Shiner happened to look up, glancing out onto the rooftop patio. He did a double take. "Boss!"

Bentine didn't believe his eyes. Standing there on the patio, flanked by two palm trees, was a youth in a red, green, and gold costume. "I want some answers from you, Bentine!" the newcomer roared.

"You'll get hot lead, chump! This is private property, and you're trespassing," Bentine hissed. "Open the door! Shiner! Shoot him!"

A shaven-headed thug hit the switch that activated the heavy glass door. As it slid open, Shiner pulled his pistol and fired off three rapid shots. Robin dived aside.

The shots missed him, and shattered a large stone planting urn. Two R-shaped throwing weapons spun from Robin's hands in rapid succession, slicing through the air and into the room. The first whacked heavily into Shiner's wrist, making him curse and drop the gun. Even before the gun hit the floor, the second whirling R slammed into the thug's forehead. He went out like a light.

An instant later Robin somersaulted into the room, his feet lashing out to strike Rake and Bandor. Before they could recover their balance, the teenager had landed. In one smooth movement his left foot came up in a powerful karate kick, knocking Bandor's legs from under him.

He'd gone easy with the thugs the other night, wary not to show too much expertise in front of the public. But here there were no onlookers to witness the harsh beating Robin administered to them. He left them groaning on the floor as he searched the penthouse.

He found Bentine trying to hide in the bedroom's walk-in closet, and hauled the gang boss out.

"Did you kill old Joe Wagner?" Robin had Bentine by the shirt front, pulling the evil little man's face close to his.

Bentine squealed like a pig in pain. "No! I swear, his death had nothing to do with me or my boys!"

"Then who did kill him?"

"You're not the cops," Bentine protested. "I don't have to tell you anything!"

Dick's grip tightened a fraction, and the gang boss winced. The teenager's grim gaze burned out of the mask he wore. "I won't ask you twice."

Bentine knew when he was beaten. "Word on the street is some robber who calls himself the Enemy might have killed him. The guy's been mugging folks around here for weeks."

"What's his real name?"

"I don't know. He wears a mask and a costume. Like you."

"Where do I find him?" Robin demanded.

"No idea. The cops pulled some suspects from the local video arcade but let them all go."

Robin's face was only a few inches from the gang boss's, but he thrust it closer still. "If you're lying," he said coldly, "I'll be back. And if I come back, it'll take a team of experienced medics a very long time to put you and your 'boys' back together again."

The teenager's gloved hand dropped from Bentine's shirt, and he turned and left without another word or a backward glance.

The arcade was a dive on Beecker Street. Robin would have preferred to go in as Dick Grayson, spend some time there before coming to a conclusion. But time was something he might not have. This "Enemy" had to be stopped before he murdered again.

The manager was a weedy little guy with a balding head, and even though he looked Robin up and down with raised eyebrows, he was too polite to mention the unusual attire. And he was happy to answer Robin's questions. It didn't take long before Nate Toomey's name cropped up.

"He's been throwing a lot of money around lately," the manager said. "My guess is, he's trying to impress the girls. Funny, though, because he doesn't have a job."

"What does he look like?" Robin wanted to know.

"Tall, strong. About seventeen years old. Black hair that sticks up in spikes whatever he does with it. Wears a leather coat, black jeans."

It was the mention of the hair that did it. Robin cast his mind back to the night Bentine came to the diner. What customers were in? Angela and her actress friends. Bill was in the corner. Several faces he didn't know . . . and yes, a teenager in a black jacket, with black spiky hair.

Using the hall phone, Robin got the Toomeys' number from the operator. Nate's mother said he wasn't in. "Try the arcade. That's where he usually goes."

But the owner said he hadn't been in all night, Robin thought, as he left the arcade's dim green lights and struck out onto the rooftops again. So . . . suppose Nate Toomey is the Enemy. Suppose he doesn't operate from home because of his parents. Then he'd have a hideout. But where? Someplace nobody goes. The derelict factory under the railway viaduct? No — too many homeless people use it for shelter. Down in the sewer network? Unlikely. The condemned apartment buildings on Delaney?

It was a stretch, but worth a try.

The Enemy munched on potato chips and waited. *I sure have learned patience since I made this costume,* he thought wryly. *I spend half my life waiting.*

He doodled idly on the timetable he held in his hand.

His plan was made. He was leaving town — but not by a route that anyone could ever trace. He'd travel over the rooftops to where the Gotham Union railway line hit a junction and branched in two separate directions. He would sneak aboard at Cliff Junction, then be over the gorge and out of the city, heading west. New Mexico, Arizona, California . . . they'd been just names to him before. Now, one of them was going to be his new home.

He wrapped the cash carefully and stuffed it in his jacket pocket. Eleven o'clock. Time to go.

He pulled his mask into place, slung his grapple and line from his belt, and climbed out the window and up onto the roof. Cautiously, he peeked over the edge. *Don't be stupid,* he chided himself. *Who'd be on a rooftop at this time of night?*

His eyes widened in surprise as a figure in red, green, and gold dropped lithely from above, landing only a few yards from him.

CHAPTER
10

I t's all over, Toomey. I know who you are."

Robin's voice was low and grim, and Nate Toomey froze. This was the last thing he'd been expecting. Police searches, yes. Roadblocks, maybe. But a guy in a costume?

Nate laughed nervously, almost a bark, before he regained his composure. "I don't know who you are, friend, but you got no business with me." He got slowly to his feet, the metal grapple fastened to its line dangling from his hand. "Now let me pass and we'll both be on our way. Otherwise, you'll find out why I call myself the Enemy."

"Very dramatic. Where were you last night?" Robin demanded. "Anywhere near Joe's Diner?"

The Enemy's eyes were hidden by his leather mask, but his body stiffened perceptibly at the words, and Robin knew that he'd found the right guy.

"What do you know about the murder of an old man?"

Robin rasped. His heart was thumping as he thought of Joe — who'd shown him so much kindness, who'd lit up so many nights with his jokes — lying cold and dead on the diner floor. More than anything else in the world, he wanted to teach this killer a lesson.

Instead of answering, the Enemy made his move. He spun the grapple, giving it an extra wrist-flick, then let it go. Robin saw it coming too late. He ducked to the side, but not fast enough. The cold metal struck him on the shoulder and bounced back as the Enemy reeled it in. Then the Enemy lashed out with a straight kick that, if it had connected cleanly, might have broken Robin's ribs. Robin rode the blow at the last moment, the Kevlar in his vest absorbing the impact, spreading its force over his whole torso.

Before Robin could recover, the Enemy was on him, fists raining down in a barrage of blows to Robin's head and shoulders. Robin covered himself as best he could, but every second another blow was finding a target. Pain shot through his whole upper body.

Robin remembered his father's advice on the trapeze — always leave your emotions on the ground. Batman had said the same thing about crimefighting. An angry fighter is a bad fighter. He makes too many mistakes. He loses the initiative.

Pity he hadn't thought of that sooner. He felt a sickening crunch on the side of his head, as the Enemy once again swung the heavy grapple at him.

"Another five minutes and I'd have been out of this stinking city," the Enemy snarled. "You can't stop me. Not now."

He shoved Robin hard. The teenager's knees buckled as they struck the low parapet that ran around the edge of the flat roof. Suddenly he lost his balance. Flailing in vain to steady himself, he went over the edge.

The Enemy stood for a second, panting with exertion. He patted his jacket to make sure the money was still safe, then ran to the other side of the roof. His grapple flashed through the air, securing itself to a metal grille in the side of the building next door. He swung through the air, on his way out of Gotham, on his way to a new life. And if the voice of his conscience had anything to say about what he'd just done, Nate wasn't in the mood for listening.

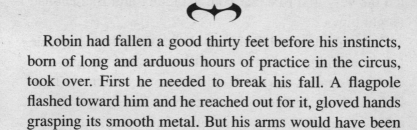

Robin had fallen a good thirty feet before his instincts, born of long and arduous hours of practice in the circus, took over. First he needed to break his fall. A flagpole flashed toward him and he reached out for it, gloved hands grasping its smooth metal. But his arms would have been ripped from their sockets if he'd clung on. He had to swing, the momentum of his body preventing the full weight of it from acting on the pole.

When his feet reached their highest point in the air, he let go. He soared toward the small stone balcony he'd targeted. But he was moving too fast to land on it. Kicking off almost as soon as his feet touched stone, he dived headfirst this time.

His hands scrabbled against a drainpipe and he fought for a grip. The pipe creaked under his weight, but it didn't give. Seconds later, he'd shinnied up and onto the roof.

There was no sign of Nate Toomey, the Enemy.

Robin had had no time to think, only react, when he'd fallen. But now that he was safe again, a dozen different sensations flooded through him: Relief that he was okay. Anger that he'd let the Enemy escape. Exhilaration at how it felt to be free and in the air once again. Disappointment that he'd let Joe down. And chagrin, because he'd forgotten the very first rule that both his father and Batman had taught him. . . .

Suddenly dejected, Robin sat down on the roof edge. He felt like a fraud. He'd trained all his life, he'd fought successfully against two of the world's worst villains — Two-Face and the Riddler — and yet he'd lost out to a rank amateur with a homemade costume and a stupid name.

It had felt so good to be in costume again, to feel that he

was doing something worthwhile . . . and now he'd failed at the very first hurdle. His ribs, arm, and face were bruised. He tasted his own blood, and a probing tongue told him that he'd loosened a tooth. He'd thought he was to be a hero again . . . and instead he'd brought disgrace on himself and the costume he wore.

He felt like giving up and slinking away into the shadows where nobody could find him and mock his pathetic efforts. *Good thing Batman doesn't know about this,* he reflected. Then he caught himself. Batman . . .

What would Batman do if this had happened to him? What would Batman do if he had lost a fight and a murderer at the same time? Robin knew the one thing he *wouldn't* do was give up. Batman hid in the shadows because it suited his task, not because he was ashamed to face the world.

Yeah — and how many times did I fall off the trapeze when I was young? Robin found himself wondering. *Dozens. But I didn't give up. I picked myself up, dusted myself off, and got right back on again, promising that I'd do better next time.*

CHAPTER
11

Brushing aside the wisps of self-pity that still clung to him, Robin got to his feet again. He'd been beaten. Okay, he'd do better next time, right? Right. So how could he make sure there would be a next time, when Nate Toomey was by his own admission on his way out of the city?

"Always analyze what clues you have," Batman had urged him when they were on the trail of Two-Face and the Riddler. Robin didn't exactly have any clues right now, unless . . .

Toomey had obviously been hiding out in the abandoned building. Maybe there was something he'd left behind.

Robin slithered on his belly until he overhung the roof edge, then reached down to grab the upper sill of a window that had long since lost its glass. Carefully, he swung himself down, taking the strain on his powerful biceps, until he stood on the window ledge. It was a simple matter to slide inside.

The building had been constructed a century earlier, to house immigrant refugees who'd flooded into Gotham to escape persecution in Europe. The apartments were small, though many had been extended and improved later. Now they were like something from a war movie. Missing fireplaces and water tanks left ugly holes in the wall, and rain had penetrated into almost every room.

All units were empty, save one. It was as bad as the others, except it had an old mattress, and there were several empty food cartons and soda bottles lying around, as if somebody had spent a lot of time here. There was a map of the city, with drawings of buildings and their access points all marked out. And there was a timetable for the trains leaving and entering the city, with a sketched map showing the railtrack through Cliff Junction.

One figure was circled in black ink — the Midnight Special, a train that blew out of Gotham on its way to New Orleans and all points west. Robin glanced at his watch — a quarter to twelve. He could still make it to the central station and find Toomey before the train pulled out on its long journey.

Seconds later he was back on the roof, facing the direction of the station, a good mile away. His line was already swinging in his hand when he thought: *Wait!* The station lay due east of here — where Robin had fallen off the ledge. But if the Enemy had swung off in that direction, Robin would have seen him. And why the sketch map of Cliff Junction?

Robin tried to remember how the railway ran. Underground to start with, then on elevated tracks as it passed through the suburbs. But the line ran near the well-lit streets, and the Enemy would risk being seen by dozens of people. What next? The train would pick up speed along the straight stretch — too fast to jump it there — before it had to slow for the Cliff Road junction and the tight turn it had to make before taking the bridge high over the tumbling Gotham River.

Of course, Robin thought. *He's going to jump the train at the junction!*

He raced to the other side of the roof, his line snaking out to secure itself around the very same grille the Enemy had used earlier. Then Robin was launching himself into space, and the city lights, the traffic below, the faint voices that drifted up — everything disappeared as he focused on his mission.

Effortlessly he swung, let go, shot his line to a new anchor point, then swung again. Sometimes his landing brought him too low, and he had to scale a fire escape or billboard to give him the height necessary to continue. Sometimes he had to race along a roof edge only inches wide, with terrifying drops to the concrete far below. But they didn't worry him at all.

Suddenly, like a clearing in a jungle, the high buildings ended, replaced by thirty or more blocks of single-story residential buildings. Hardly possible to swing from rooftop to rooftop there — and running along the street in full view wasn't exactly good crimefighter style.

Swiftly Robin dropped from the ledge to gargoyle to flagpole to low roof, finally vaulting from a second-floor fire escape to land lightly on top of a passing late-night bus. There was only one place it could be heading for in this direction — the Cliff Road station.

Robin took the free ride all the way, along with the few passengers aboard who were heading for home in the small project nearby. As the bus slowed to enter the depot where it would turn, Robin's line shot out to catch hold of a nearby oak tree. Then he was gone, disappearing into the branches.

The tree stood at the bottom of a high, steep embankment along which the railway line ran. Robin intended to drop to the ground, then run back along the foot of the slope to the actual junction, where he guessed the Enemy would make his move. He glanced at his watch: a few minutes after midnight. He could already hear the steady beat of the locomotive as the train pulled out of the city and came quickly closer.

Robin saw its lights as it emerged from behind some warehouses. When he saw what was illuminated in the train's beam, he cursed. He'd guessed wrong!

The tracks ran alongside a building site, and silhouetted atop the boom of the squat crane that stood there was the Enemy. The boom jutted out only a yard or so higher than the train top, and the villain had an easy drop to the train roof. As the train rumbled below him, he jumped carefully, rolled, and clung close to the roof. A smug grin widened under his mask.

He'd done it! He was out of this city, on his way to better things. Three thousand dollars was a lot of money, but it wouldn't last long. He wasn't bothered. He knew what he could do, and what he did in Gotham, he could do anywhere else in America. He could mug people, and stick up stores, and make himself a real good living. He just needed to plan things, select the right jobs, the ones that paid the most for the least effort and risk.

Maybe he'd drop a card to his mother and father telling them how well he was doing. Then again, maybe he wouldn't. He wasn't going to miss them and their nagging, and their dull, tedious lives. Nate Toomey was going places! If he played this right, he could become a very rich guy indeed. For the first time since he'd struck the old man in the diner, the Enemy relaxed.

As the train steamed toward him, Robin knew he could never drop to the ground, run up the banking, come alongside it, and leap aboard. It was going too fast, the banking too steep. He was going to lose his quarry again!

Unless . . .

Even as he thought of it, he knew he'd do it. Just above his head the tree trunk split into two forks. The larger went straight up, but the other branched out at a steep angle until its top overhung the tracks. Urgently, Robin climbed higher, out along the branching limb. In the darkness he was prodded and ripped by a dozen small, unseen twigs, but gamely he forced his way through them. The branch's very end stretched out over the railway tracks — but a good twenty feet higher than the top of the train.

It was a long drop onto a moving target, and the train's speed meant he'd have to judge his landing to perfection or be thrown violently off. He could be seriously injured. Or worse.

Robin took a deep breath, consciously relaxing his entire body. With a monstrous roar the train charged by below him in a blur. It was now or never. He dropped.

He landed in a crouch slightly off center of the third car, arms spread wide in an attempt to keep his balance. He'd have done it, too, if the train hadn't lurched suddenly as it changed tracks. Jerked off-balance, Robin toppled over to his left, hands scrabbling for purchase on the roof as he tried desperately to avoid being thrown off.

He succeeded, his gauntlets managing to obtain a hold on the low line of rivets that ran up the center of the roof. Just in time, for his feet and lower legs were already hanging out over the edge. He stayed as still as he could, only the grip of his fingers stopping him from being thrown off completely.

"Didn't learn the first time, eh?"

Robin's heart stopped. He had been so intent on saving himself that he hadn't seen the Enemy approach.

The train lurched again as the automatic signal switched it onto new tracks, and suddenly they were on the Highwater Bridge. Out of the corner of his eye, Robin could see the surging rapids as the river raged over the rock-strewn bottleneck gorge two hundred feet below.

"No more chances!" The Enemy raised his foot and stamped down on Robin's hand. He grunted with pain, fingers clutching to retain what little grip they had. He couldn't fight back from this position — and he couldn't stand many more stamps like that before he'd have to let go. He'd arc down through space to smash off the gorge's rocky walls before vanishing into the torrent below.

He had only one slim chance, and he took it. At the very moment the Enemy stamped down on his right hand, Robin let go with his left and grabbed. For a wild moment he thought he'd misjudged it. He felt his body starting to slide away over the edge of the train. But then his fingers grabbed the Enemy's ankle.

As the Enemy fell back off-balance, Robin used his foe's own weight as an anchor to swing himself back onto the roof of the train.

They rolled to their feet as one, both angling to strike the other. But it was Robin's punch that connected first. It took the Enemy in the midriff, and he grunted and fell back. Robin pivoted, allowing for the motion of the swaying train. His foot came up in a powerful karate kick that caught the Enemy hard on the thigh and made him stumble to his knees.

But the Enemy recovered fast, already rising to his feet again as Robin closed with him. They locked arms like wrestlers, each straining and maneuvering for the best advantage of the grip.

"You're a fool," the Enemy hissed, his voice raw. Up

close, the mask gave him a near-demonic look. "I'm going to kill you now!"

"It takes more than a homemade mask to frighten me, creep," Robin shot back. His muscles bulged as he fought to force the other's arms back. "I know you for what you are — a parasite! You feast on people weaker than you, people who can't fight back, people who work hard to get the money you steal from them!"

"It's the law of the jungle! The strong eat the weak!"

The veins in Robin's forehead bulged with effort. "We're not animals," he said emphatically. "We're human beings."

They strained against each other, constantly making tiny adjustments to their balance because of the moving train.

"I am the Enemy! I prey on weaklings like you!"

"Is that so?" Robin wasn't impressed. "Well, I'm Robin. Remember the name. I stop people like you in their tracks!"

The engine had reached the end of the bridge, and its whistle gave out a long, lonely cry. Below, gnarled pine trees grew out of the cliff face, their ancient roots dug deep into the crumbling rock. And below them, almost straight down, a wall of water raged, the river's last outburst before it calmed and ran into the sea.

Without warning, Robin relaxed his grip and fell back. The Enemy was thrown forward by the momentum of his own effort. He gasped as Robin's feet came up to take him solidly in the chest. Then he was being hefted through the air, to slam onto the roof again on his back.

Though he was winded, the Enemy wasn't finished yet. As Robin turned to face him, the villain snatched his grapple from his waist and whirled it. It shot straight at Robin's face. But the teenager ducked and the grapple sailed on into a branch of an overhanging tree. Suddenly the line went taut as the train sped on. Wound around the Enemy's wrist, the line jerked him forcefully into the air. For a second he hung there — and then the line snapped.

Robin raced along the carriage roof, his own line in his hand. But even if he threw it and lassoed his falling foe, the Enemy could still be killed as he was bounced off the cliff face and dragged along after the train. Robin wanted him captured, not killed. He wanted justice, not execution.

Robin's eyes drank in the whole scene below him as his legs tensed and he flung himself off the train, plunging headfirst after the Enemy. There was a tree halfway down — rotten branches — but if it held . . .

Robin reached out an arm and grabbed the Enemy around the waist. His other hand sent his line curling out, the weighted R-symbol curving like a flying saucer as it snaked up and around a branch. It snapped into place, the duo dropped past it, and the line grew taut.

Robin heard the sharp crack as the branch broke, but he

was already swinging, using their momentum to launch them to safety.

They landed in the branches of an aged and gnarled pine, its sharp needles digging into their exposed flesh. The Enemy made a last futile effort to win the fight, weakly drawing back his fist to take a swing at his savior.

But the Boy Wonder had had enough. "No more chances for *you!*" he proclaimed, and his own fist crashed into the Enemy's jaw. "Lights out!"

The Enemy sagged against him, and Robin breathed a sigh of relief. It was over. Later, he might think of what he'd done and shudder at the breathtaking audacity of it. But now he was just relieved. He was alive, the Enemy had been caught, and he hadn't let old Joe down.

He knew that he'd reached a turning point in his life. He'd chosen what he wanted to do. And he'd done it.

Now all I have to do, he thought with a wry smile, *is figure out how to get myself and my prisoner out of a tree fifty feet above a whirlpool and up the slope to the railway, then walk the four miles back into Gotham.*

It was going to be a long night!

CHAPTER
12

Midnight. Blackgate Prison Island rose out of Gotham Sound like a castle from an ogre's nightmare. The gaunt, bleak building seemed to merge with the island's living rock to form one grim, unwelcoming mass. Waves reared up and crashed against the rugged cliffs. Towers and turrets clawed blindly at the sky, lit here and there by the permanent searchlights that scoured the prison walls.

A cold wind whistled in off the sea, and the prison guards were glad to be secure behind the double-glazed, bulletproof windows of their towers. Winter was just beginning. Old prisoners said that, come January, the winds were cold enough to strip men's flesh from their bones.

In his cell, Nate Toomey sat huddled in a threadbare prison blanket, staring grimly out of his barred window. He couldn't sleep. He hadn't been able to sleep since he first arrived here, and the harsh reality of his future had come home to him.

Ten years, he was thinking bitterly. *Ten years of my life to be wasted on this freezing, stinking rock! And why? Because some do-gooder stuck his nose in my business!*

Slowly his fingers closed, as if he were strangling the life out of an imaginary Robin. There was no thought in his head for his victims, for the people he'd hurt and used and cheated. And killed. He hated them all. All those decent, ordinary people with their decent, ordinary lives, while he was cooped up here in an escape-proof jail. But most of all he hated Robin. In his mind, all the blame for his own predicament lay squarely on the shoulders of the Boy Wonder.

"One day I'll get out of here," he vowed softly. "One day I'll find you, Robin. And I swear I'll make you pay!"

Nate Toomey hadn't learned anything at all.

Midnight. The air was chilly now, the skies above Gotham lit by the glow from millions of lights, blotting out all but the brightest stars.

Down on the streets, the crowds from the late-night theaters spilled out into the cold and began to disperse. Men turned up their collars and women snuggled into their coats as they hurried for the welcome warmth inside their cars or taxis. Not one of them looked up, so none saw the lone figure perched atop a gargoyle forty stories above, his slender silhouette etched against the moon.

Balanced confidently, the figure gazed out over the city. He was no longer Dick Grayson. With the mask in place, wearing the costume of red, green, and gold, he was Robin now. A sea of lights twinkled as far as he could see in all directions. Gotham was a mighty city. He thought of the millions of people, all going about their business, all making what they could of their lives . . . and the corners of his mouth turned down with distaste as he remembered the parasites who prey on them.

His own life had turned to tragedy, but now he had the ability to help others, to prevent the same grief befalling them.

He turned slightly as Batman stepped from the rooftop shadows where he'd been all but invisible.

The older man looked at the teenager for a moment, then put a fatherly hand on his shoulder.

"Remember what I once told you," he said softly. "We can never go back. Survivors must go forward."

Robin nodded. "I know. I've learned a lot in the past few weeks. Like, crimefighting isn't a game. And heroes aren't made — they make themselves."

"You found yourself, then?" Batman asked. "I hoped that you would. I'm glad that you did." He reached out a gloved hand. "Perhaps now we really can be partners."

Partners. The word sounded good to Robin. He grinned as he put out his own hand, and they clasped. He knew that a corner had been turned. He had grown up. He had a reason for going on. When he helped others, his own pain was forgotten. He could make a difference. For the good.

He and Batman were on the same wavelength now. He understood why Batman did what he did. And he knew too that now he, Robin, must do the same. Almost like destiny, though it was no fluke of blind fate, because he had made the choice himself.

The weighted R on the end of his throwing line swirled out through the night air. "What are we waiting for, partner? There are a million criminals out there. Let's go catch us a few!" The line snapped taut around a flagpole, and Robin launched himself into the night.

For a fleeting instant, if any of the hunched and scurrying shapes below had looked up, they'd have seen two shadows pass fleetingly across the face of the moon. Batman and Robin were back in business.

And as they disappeared into the darkness, like living shadows, the wind whipped around and seemed to whisper to the night: "A hero is reborn."

ABOUT THE AUTHOR

ALAN GRANT was born in Bristol, England, in 1949. His grandmother taught him to read at the age of three, using *Batman* and other adventure comics as her textbooks, and he has been a comics fanatic ever since. Leaving school when he was seventeen to pursue a career in accounting, he quickly realized he'd made a mistake and switched to publishing. After editing wildlife, romance, and fashion magazines, he quit to go freelance and produced a successful run of teenage true confession stories before returning to his first love: comics. With longtime writing partner John Wagner, he scripted *Judge Dredd* and a dozen other science fiction series for the British comic book sensation *2000AD*. This work brought him to the attention of *Batman* editor Dennis O'Neil, and in the nine years since then, Alan has written more than a hundred different Batman stories. He is currently the regular writer of

Batman: Shadow of the Bat (sixty-five issues and counting!) and *Lobo* for DC Comics, and is working on a top-secret project with John Wagner and fan-favorite artist Simon Bisley. His previous two Batman novels — *Batman: Knightfall & Beyond* and *Batman Forever* — were both bestsellers. Alan lives and works in a Gothic mansion in the Scottish border country with his wife and guardian angel, Sue.

THE ADVENTURES NEVER END IN GOTHAM CITY.

SUBSCRIBE TODAY!

Choose any of these action-packed titles
and receive 12 monthly issues:

Retail price: $21.00

YOU PAY: $16.00

☐ **Adventures in the DC Universe**
☐ **Batman & Robin Adventures**
☐ **Impulse** ☐ **Robin**
☐ **Superman Adventures**

DIRECTIONS FOR APPLYING TATTOOS:
1. Cut out the tattoo you wish to apply.
2. Lightly wet skin with soapy water.
3. Place tattoo facedown on the wet area.
4. Press down for 5 seconds.
5. Remove paper.
   Tattoo can be removed by using soap, water, and a washcloth.

DIRECTIONS FOR APPLYING TATTOOS:
1. Cut out the tattoo you wish to apply.
2. Lightly wet skin with soapy water.
3. Place tattoo facedown on the wet area.
4. Press down for 5 seconds.
5. Remove paper.
   Tattoo can be removed by using soap, water, and a washcloth.

DIRECTIONS FOR APPLYING TATTOOS:
1. Cut out the tattoo you wish to apply.
2. Lightly wet skin with soapy water.
3. Place tattoo facedown on the wet area.
4. Press down for 5 seconds.
5. Remove paper.
   Tattoo can be removed by using soap, water, and a washcloth.

DIRECTIONS FOR APPLYING TATTOOS:
1. Cut out the tattoo you wish to apply.
2. Lightly wet skin with soapy water.
3. Place tattoo facedown on the wet area.
4. Press down for 5 seconds.
5. Remove paper.
   Tattoo can be removed by using soap, water, and a washcloth.

DIRECTIONS FOR APPLYING TATTOOS:
1. Cut out the tattoo you wish to apply.
2. Lightly wet skin with soapy water.
3. Place tattoo facedown on the wet area.
4. Press down for 5 seconds.
5. Remove paper.
   Tattoo can be removed by using soap, water, and a washcloth.

DIRECTIONS FOR APPLYING TATTOOS:
1. Cut out the tattoo you wish to apply.
2. Lightly wet skin with soapy water.
3. Place tattoo facedown on the wet area.
4. Press down for 5 seconds.
5. Remove paper.
   Tattoo can be removed by using soap, water, and a washcloth.

INGREDIENTS: Hydroxypropyl Methylcellulose. May also contain FD&C Yellow #5, FD&C Yellow #6, FD&C Blue #1 and D&C Red #28. All ink colorants are FDA certified and non-toxic.